# From Nature
# By Esme

N.K. Lazarre

N.K. Lazarre Books

# DEDICATION

For my son who is forever my source of inspiration, my mother who fills my spirit with creativity even though she is no longer here, my father who shows me what can be achieved through hard work, my talented brother who is my example for what is possible, and my wonderful husband whose encouragement and support are endless.

"And for those of us who take the time to embrace her lessons, may we be selfless and kind enough to pass them on."

-   **Esme**

January 1

"Nature"

Dear Reader,

Every year, I start a brand-new journal. I've always loved to write. Before, I only wrote for myself. But this year, I thought how wonderful it would be to write entries that I could share with others.

This past year has been a real tough one. My mom has always told me to try and keep a positive attitude. She has said that instead of looking at what I don't have, look at what I do have and appreciate the small gifts in life that are filled with love and hope. These are the things that will help keep me grounded in times of uncertainty.

With everything that's been going on lately, life has felt like a whirlwind. But when I slow down and really pay attention to nature, I find a calm stillness. And in the quiet, I feel awake, curious, connected, and grateful.

What I have observed is everything in nature is different; this makes each thing stand out. These same differences equip all things for survival and unify them with the common goal of maintaining nature's delicate balance.

I feel that nature is not just here for us to admire. She wants us to stop, take notice, and learn.

And for those of us who take the time to embrace her lessons, may we be selfless and kind enough to pass them on.

Learn.

Love,
Esme

January 4

"Light"

Dear Reader,

Have you ever heard of the word bioluminescence? Bioluminescence is a big word that to me, has an even bigger meaning. It is a chemical process that makes living organisms give off light.

Think of the glow of fireflies. That is bioluminescence at work. It turns out that fireflies are not the only organisms that are able to produce their own light. There are fungi, fish, bacteria, jellyfish, and lots of other creatures on land and in the ocean that can glow too.

Now these organisms do not have this ability just to have it, they have it for a reason. Some organisms use it for hunting prey, some use it to defend themselves, and some use it to find a mate. There are even animals that depend on the bioluminescence of other organisms to help them survive. There is a whale species that hunts in areas full of bioluminescent plankton. When a fish swims up to eat the plankton, the plankton start glowing like tiny warning lights. That glow alerts the whale, who swoops in and eats the fish. The whale gets a meal, and the plankton stay safe. A win for both the whale and plankton.

As humans, we do not produce a light that is visible to the naked eye but that does not mean that we can't shine. We all have an inner light that is shaped by our spirit, purpose, and the way that we see the world.

When we try to understand things with a positive attitude and a hopeful mindset, we start noticing what's true, beautiful, and good.

And when life gets hard, that inner light lets us brighten a dark moment, not just for ourselves, but for other people too.

Shine.

Love,
Esme

January 10

"Host"

Dear Reader,

Virology is the study of viruses. A virus is a tiny organism, so tiny you can't see it without a microscope. There are tons of different viruses in the world. Some you've probably heard of, and others you might not know at all. For example, influenza, more commonly known as "the flu", is caused by a virus.

Even though viruses can be different from one another, they all work in a similar way. They enter our bodies, copy themselves, and spread. One important thing about viruses is that they can't survive on their own; they need a living host to do so.

Viruses usually get into our bodies through places like our nose or mouth. Once they're in, they attach to one of our cells and inject their genetic material into it. Then they trick the cells into making more copies of themselves and pretty soon one tiny virus turns into many. The symptoms we get, like coughing or sneezing, are actually ways the virus uses our bodies to help it spread to someone else.

Hate works kind of like a virus: it can't survive on its own, it only grows when it lives inside someone, and it can spread from person to person. But here's the difference; unlike a real virus, we have a choice in being filled with and passing on hate. Instead of hate, choose to be a host to something positively infectious.

Spread Joy.

Love,
Esme

January 15

"Roots"

Dear Reader,

Plants and trees all have root systems. Their roots pull water and nutrients from the soil, keep them steady as they grow, and help hold the soil together so it doesn't blow or wash away.

People have roots too. Sometimes "roots" mean our family history, but it can also mean the things that ground us and make us feel stable. When I'm facing something new or challenging, I can feel unsure, frustrated, or insecure; sometimes all three at once. Life is full of unexplored places and first-time experiences. Life pushes us out of our comfort zone on purpose, so we can stretch and grow. And just like a tree, we need a strong foundation to anchor us and help support our own growth.

During uncertain times, root yourself in belief, purpose, hope, and love. Look at new experiences as chances to learn. Trust the process of living and learning, even when you don't understand everything right away.

When life shifts and circumstances change, stay grounded in your purpose so you don't get blown off course.

And remember to always water yourself with hope. Let it help your dreams grow and your motivation deepen. When you do that, you will never run out of inner strength, and you will keep growing from the inside out.

Anchor.

Love,
Esme

January 18

"Community"

Dear Reader,

I came across a quote by Leonardo da Vinci that really stuck with me. It reads, "The men of experiment are like the ant; they only collect and use. But the bee gathers its materials from the flowers of the garden and of the field, but transforms and digests it by the power of its own."

When honey bees collect nectar and pollen from a flower, the pollen they carry helps other flowers grow new seeds. The nectar they gather gets turned into honey, which becomes food for young bees in the hive. They mix nectar and pollen to make bee pollen, sometimes called bee bread, which they feed to the larvae. In each of these examples, the bee begins with something from nature and turns it into something new. Bees don't just take, they create, and they give back in abundance. What one bee gathers will nourish and strengthen many others.

Within the hive, bees have specific roles that are important for the survival of the colony and each bee uses its own set of skills for the good of the whole. Because of this, bees represent community, cooperation, hard work, and productivity.

Each of us has our own set of unique skills and talents. Some we might not have discovered yet, and others we may know we have but aren't sure how to use them. Keep searching for them, practicing them, and exploring them, because like the bee we all have the potential to create something meaningful and useful to share with others.

Nourish.

Love,
Esme

February 7

"Perspective"

Dear Reader,

A prism is a solid shape - usually made of glass - with two matching, parallel ends and flat sides. From the outside, a prism looks simple. But when you hold it up to the light, it reveals something completely unexpected; a full spectrum of colors hidden inside a single beam of white light. The same thing happens in nature when light passes through tiny water droplets and a rainbow is revealed. The only difference is that we can't control when nature creates a rainbow, but if we have a prism, we can make a rainbow at any time just by holding it in the right place so that light can shine through it.

A prism is the perfect metaphor for understanding a perspective that's different from our own. Some ideas or opinions might seem straightforward when we first look at them - maybe even too simple to understand why someone else sees them differently. But when we hold that perspective up to the light - meaning we give it space, attention, and an honest chance - we start to see the layers within it. We see the experiences behind it, the feelings connected to it, and the meaning that wasn't obvious at first glance.

The prism teaches us that truth isn't always found on the surface. Sometimes we have to adjust the angle, be open to the light, and let understanding pass through us before a fuller, more colorful picture appears.

By being willing to "shift the prism", we can reveal the true meaning behind someone else's point of view and grow in the process.

Shift.

Love,
Esme

February 14

"Foundation"

Dear Reader,

Happy Valentine's Day! Today felt like the perfect day to write about love. Love is a powerful feeling. It doesn't just make us happy, it helps take care of us, too.

Scientists say love can actually be good for our hearts. There are many kinds of love in the world: love from family, friends, partners, and even the love we give ourselves. Spending time with people who make us feel safe and supported, choosing kindness, and practicing self-love can help lower stress and keep our hearts healthy. That's probably why the heart is the symbol of love, because our hearts truly grow stronger when they are cared for.

Every relationship needs a strong foundation. Adélie and Gentoo penguins show this in a beautiful way. When a male penguin is courting, he offers a pebble to a female. If she accepts it, they use that pebble to help build their nest - a sturdy home made from many small stones.

Our relationships are built the same way. Our "stones" are love, kindness, acceptance, and respect. These are the pieces that hold everything together. And it all begins with you. When you place those stones in your own life first, you create a strong foundation inside yourself. Once your foundation is solid, you're ready to offer stones to others and build something lasting together.

Build.

Love,
Esme

February 20

"Above"

Dear Reader,

You've probably heard the saying, "you can't see the forest for the trees." While it's true that trees can block your view of the rest of the forest, this saying isn't really about trees - it's about perspective. It means we can get so focused on the details that are right in front of us that we don't look at the bigger picture. And the ironic part? Focusing only on the details that are in your immediate view can actually make a problem feel bigger or hinder you from solving it at all.

There are lots of reasons that this can happen. Sometimes a problem feels overwhelming because there are too many details at once - or not enough - and we don't know where to start. Other times, we assume a situation is the same as something we've experienced before, so we only focus on the details we recognize. And sometimes, when we've never dealt with a specific type of problem, we limit ourselves to what's obvious and don't try to look beyond it. When I experience either of these, I step back and take a bird's-eye view.

Birds are pretty amazing. They can move at different speeds, fly at different heights, and handle all kinds of weather. The view a bird has while sitting in a tree is completely different from the view it has while soaring high in the sky. From up there, it can see for miles. It's kind of like being in an airplane - at first you only see buildings and trees, but once you're in the air, everything opens up and you can see so much more.

When you feel stuck in the details and can only see the trees, imagine lifting off and looking down from above.

That wider view can help you to not just see the forest, but all the paths that can lead you through it.

Rise.

Love,
Esme

February 28

"Axis"

Dear Reader,

When people talk about night and day, they are usually referring to things that are opposite of one another. You might even hear someone say that two people are "as different as night and day."

Night and day happen because the Earth is always rotating on its axis. When one side of the Earth faces the sun, it's daytime there. When it turns away from the sun, that same place experiences night.

Daylight brings brightness and warmth to help wake us up. Just like plants, we're energized by the sun as we grow to take on the responsibilities and challenges of the day. Along with other daytime creatures, we move through our routines, trying to get everything done before the light fades.

Night arrives with a quieter kind of strength. While we sleep, our bodies recover from the day and get ready for what's next. Plants and animals that rest during the day come alive, and stars that were once hidden sparkle in the night sky.

It's easy to compare night and day and even prefer one over the other. But I appreciate both because together, they show balance in nature. We need both light and darkness for life on Earth to thrive.

In the same way that day and night create balance in nature, we can create balance for one another. Just as the Earth turns on its axis, humanity turns on an axis of compassion and connection.

When we work together for the greater good, we can help make sure that no one is left in the dark - and that everyone gets a chance to stand in the light.

Turn.

Love,
Esme

March 1

"Flight"

Dear Reader,

Today, I saw a hummingbird sipping nectar from a flower. It was right there in front of me, so close I felt like I could reach out and touch it. As it hovered in the air, its wings beat so fast they completely blurred into the background. For a moment, it almost looked wingless, like its tiny body was just floating. The only sign of the presence of its wings was the soft humming sound they made as they fluttered.

There are more than 300 species of hummingbirds. Most of them are only about three to five inches long and weigh around four grams. That's about the weight of a nickel. The smallest species, called the bee hummingbird, is just about two inches long from beak to tail and weighs less than two grams, which is lighter than a penny.

Even though they're small and delicate, hummingbirds are incredibly powerful. Their hearts are huge compared to their bodies, making up about 2.5 percent of their total weight, and their chest and wing muscles account for about ten percent. Because of this, they can flap their wings an unbelievable 50 to 80 times per second. During migration, they can travel incredible distances, sometimes flying up to 500 miles in less than a day.

Hummingbirds are mostly solitary. While flying they can reach speeds of 25 to 35 miles per hour and dive as fast as 60 miles per hour. But it's not just their speed that's impressive. They're also incredibly agile, able to hover, fly forward, backward, and even upside down.

It's amazing that a bird so small can do so many extraordinary things. They are proof that ability isn't defined by size, it's defined by determination. When others doubt you, believe in yourself and trust in your own abilities. Let the hummingbird remind you to be brave, because sometimes you will need to fly alone and to the sound of your own hum.

Soar.

Love,
Esme

March 7

"Shed"

Dear Reader,

Snakes don't have the best reputation, and I'll admit that there was a time when I wasn't a fan of them either. But I've learned that every creature has a purpose and can teach us something meaningful about life.

Snakes are especially interesting because they're the only animals that can shed their entire outer skin layer in one large single piece. Unlike humans and most other animals, a snake's skin doesn't grow with its body. When it outgrows its skin, it has to leave the old one behind. It's kind of like when your clothes get too small and you have to get a bigger size.

The skin a snake sheds can actually tell us a lot. From it, we can learn the snake's age, what kind of snake it is, and even clues about its health. Since snakes are territorial, the presence of shedded skin can also be a sign that one might be close by!

Today I watched a snake resting on a warm rock. Nearby I found its old skin - thin, papery, and curled like it had been gently unbuttoned. It was at this moment that I realized something important. The snake shed its skin because it had grown on the inside. The old skin couldn't stretch any farther, so it had to be left behind. It didn't lose itself - it made room for itself.

I think people are a little like that too. When we learn, heal, or become braver, it happens quietly inside us first. One day, the old way of being doesn't fit anymore. When we let it go, we aren't becoming someone new - we are giving ourselves space to become stronger and better versions of ourselves.

Nature reminds us that change isn't about turning into someone else, it's about growing enough so that we are ready and able to move forward.

Change.

Love,
Esme

March 10

"Patience"

Dear Reader,

I am not always a patient person. To be honest, patience is still something I have to practice every day. But I think it's better to be a work in progress than to make no progress at all. Before I write about patience, I want to write about its opposite - impatience.

Impatience happens when we treat time like an enemy instead of a friend. It makes us rush toward the end of a moment instead of being fully present in it. We fear time slipping away, rather than trusting the small, steady way it moves us forward. When we are impatient, we feel as though we are always behind time - chasing it to catch up with it instead of moving alongside it. Pearls always remind me of the beauty of patience.

Pearls are made when something irritating - often a tiny parasite - finds its way into a mollusk like an oyster, mussel, or clam. The mollusk can't push it out so it protects itself by covering the irritant with a smooth, shining substance called nacre. Layer by layer, over many months - and sometimes years - a pearl is formed. Small pearls can take about six months, while larger ones can take up to four years.

I like to imagine that we are the mollusk, and patience is the pearl. At first, time can feel irritating and uncomfortable. But when we stop fighting it and learn to work with it, something beautiful begins to form. With each passing moment, patience gains another layer, slowly growing in strength and shine.

Time gives us wisdom, experience, and space to heal. When we choose to live inside each moment -every minute, every hour, every day - we allow those layers to build.

Just like with a pearl, time and layers give patience its depth and luster. But unlike a pearl, whose value is measured in money, patience is a treasure that is truly priceless.

Grow.

Love,
Esme

March 15

"Show"

Dear Reader,

There are more than 400,000 species of flowering plants in the world. Like people, flowers come in all different colors, shapes, and sizes. When they bloom, they don't hide. They open fully, letting their colors show; gently inviting our eyes to notice their beauty.

Sometimes I think it's interesting that we celebrate how different flowers are, but don't always do the same for each other. Being judged for simply being yourself can make it hard to open up. It can make you want to stay closed and small. When I feel that way, I imagine myself as a flower bud. A bud always blooms. If it didn't, the beauty inside it would never be seen.

One of my favorite flowers is the *Peniocereus greggii*, also called the *Night-blooming Cereus* or *Queen of the Night*. It's a cactus flower found in Arizona, New Mexico, and parts of Mexico. Its bloom is white and delicate, and it opens only at night - just once a year, usually in June or July. The bloom is also short, lasting only a few hours. What amazes me most is that all the flowers in an area bloom at the same time, almost as if they are standing together in quiet solidarity. No one fully understands why this happens, not even scientists.

When the *Queen of the Night* blooms, people gather just to witness it. For a brief moment, everyone is connected by wonder. I like to think this is nature's way of reminding us that beauty can bring us all together.

In a world full of flowers, the *Peniocereus greggii* is rare and unforgettable. Once you see it bloom, it stays with you.

Don't be afraid to be different. Don't be afraid to stand out. Don't be afraid to be completely and unmistakably you. The ones who truly care will show up. They will take the time to get to know you and embrace you exactly as you are.

Bloom.

Love,
Esme

March 25

"Impact"

Dear Reader,

I've learned that I can't control how others treat me, but I can choose how I treat others. The Golden Rule says to "treat others the way you want to be treated". But I've realized what feels acceptable to me might not feel the same to someone else. If I only measure my actions by my own comfort, I might miss how they truly make others feel.

Instead, I try to pause and imagine the impact of my actions. Even when there may be no visible consequences for me, there are always consequences - positive or negative - for the person on the receiving end. How we treat others leaves a mark, whether we choose to see it or not.

This lesson, I learned from nature by looking at coral reefs. Reefs are built by tiny coral polyps that cluster together and create strong structures from calcium carbonate. Coral reefs are some of the most diverse ecosystems on Earth, providing shelter for nearly a quarter of all marine species. They also protect coastlines from storms and erosion and help support life far beyond the reef itself.

But coral reefs are delicate. Small changes in water temperature, nutrients, or chemicals can cause them great harm. Pollution, plastic debris, climate change, dredging, and even chemicals from sunscreen have all contributed to their decline. Human actions, some unintentional, have left lasting effects on these ecosystems.

People are similar to reefs in that we are diverse, complex, and sensitive in different ways. While our needs may vary, one thing remains the same; how we treat each other matters; our actions can either support growth and safety - or quietly cause harm. As subtle changes can damage an entire reef - our words and behaviors can deeply affect others, even when our impact feels small to us.

Recognize.

Love,
Esme

April 4

"Strengths"

Dear Reader,

The Cheetah has always been one of my favorite animals. Like many, I admire cheetahs for their speed. They are the fastest land animals in the world and can go from 0 to 70 mph in a few seconds. But cheetahs don't just run fast, they are built for speed.

Their bodies are slim and streamlined, with narrow heads and shoulders and lightweight bones that reduce resistance and allow the cheetah to move through the air with ease. A long body, long legs, and an incredibly flexible spine allow the cheetah to stretch into full stride, lifting all four paws off the ground at once. With each stride, they can cover a remarkable amount of distance in very little time. Their long tails help them balance and change direction quickly, while the rough pads on the bottom of their paws and their non-retractable claws help them grip the ground for traction. From head to toe, everything about a cheetah serves its ability to run.

Yet, what impresses me most about the cheetah isn't just how fast it can go - it is its knowing how to best use its speed. A cheetah can only sprint for short bursts before becoming exhausted. To make up for its lack of endurance, the cheetah is very strategic. When hunting it waits, observes, and moves at the right moment. Teaching us to honor our strengths, embrace each opportunity, and move with intention.

Honor.

Love,
Esme

April 19

"Forward"

Dear Reader,

There are always signs that tell us when spring has arrived. The days stretch a little longer. Birds fill the air with song. Flowers appear where there was once quiet ground, and animals step out from their winter rest. If winter is a blank canvas, then spring is an artist at work, patiently creating a masterpiece. Each year, we are lucky enough to witness her unveiling.

Seeds are scattered everywhere. Nature doesn't work alone getting the seeds to new locations - she invites help from passing animals, the wind, flowing water, and even people. The warmth and gentle rains create the perfect conditions for the seeds to take hold. Seeds become flowers, flowers create more seeds, and the cycle continues. It feels like nature is always paying her gifts forward.

This is how nature gives - freely and without hesitation. And when she gives, she includes others in the process. Sometimes the real gift isn't the flower that eventually blooms, but the sharing of the seeds long before they ever touch the soil.

It's a quiet reminder of how one small act can multiply into something much larger, spreading beauty far beyond where it began.

Give.

Love,
Esme

April 23

"Faith"

Dear Reader,

I think one of the most memorable moments from the movie *Charlotte's Web* has always been the ending. I can still picture the spiderlings crawling out of the egg sac, releasing their silken threads, and lifting into the air as the wind carried them away. When I was younger, I wondered what happened to them? How far did they travel? Did they land safely? Where did they spin their own webs? Did they find a friend like Wilbur? Did they inherit Charlotte's gift of words? The scene left me with so many questions.

As I've grown older, this scene has always reminded me how life is filled with unknowns. It often requires us to take a step forward without knowing exactly where we will end up; gently nudging us to embrace discovery as a part of our own journey.

What the spiderlings did at the end of the movie is called ballooning. Once the wind caught their silk strands, it would determine how far they would travel and where they would eventually land; guiding them as they set out in search of new resources.

While we can't always control where life carries us, we can choose how we look at where it takes us. Faith isn't about knowing every answer or seeing the full path ahead. It's about trusting that wherever we land, possibility awaits us.

Believe.

Love,
Esme

April 30

"Space"

Dear Reader,

It is easy to place value in things. Outside pressures can make us feel as though we need to count what we own, compare what we have to what others have, and even measure ourselves by what's missing. Without realizing it, we start valuing possessions more than people. I don't think wanting things is wrong, but I do think it's important to be careful about what we let take up space in our lives.

Marsupials are mammals found in Australasia and the Americas. These mammals carry their young in a pouch; holding them close until they are ready for the world. Kangaroos, koalas, wombats, and opossums all depend on their pouch to protect what is most important. If it were filled with excess, there would be no room for new life to grow.

I think our lives work in much the same way. When we fill them with too much "stuff", we leave little room for ourselves, and for the people and moments that truly matter. The most valuable things are never objects; they are the relationships we nurture, the moments we hold close, and the values we carry with us wherever we go.

So I try to be mindful of what I hold on to. I strive to fill my life with meaning, connection, and care. These are the things that are always worth making space for.

Save.

Love,
Esme

May 5

"Change"

Dear Reader,

When people talk about butterflies, they often begin with the caterpillar. The contrast between how a butterfly starts and where it ends up is so striking that it has become a symbol of transformation. The visible change is the part we notice most - the wings, the colors, and the ability for flight. What impresses me most is not just the transformation itself, but the quiet preparation that makes it all possible.

A butterfly's life moves through four distinct stages: egg, caterpillar, chrysalis, and adult. When the caterpillar first hatches from the egg, it immediately begins working. It eats steadily, nourishing itself on leaves, growing from one version of itself to another. Each time its skin becomes too small, it sheds it, making room for growth. During this time, the caterpillar is not only sustaining itself for the present; it is quietly preparing for what it will one day become.

When it has taken in all that it needs, the caterpillar stops, finds a safe place beneath a leaf or branch, and wraps itself in a silk cocoon. Inside the chrysalis, a new transformation takes place. The energy stored earlier is now used to build wings, legs, eyes and all of the parts of the adult butterfly. In time, the butterfly emerges, pauses to rest, then continues the cycle by laying eggs of its own.

It's amazing how instinct guides every step. The female butterfly knows exactly which plant to place her eggs on. The caterpillar eats just enough to prepare for the next stage. Inside the chrysalis, growth continues even though it can't be seen. And once the butterfly emerges, it waits patiently while its wings unfold and harden before it ever tries to fly.

Change, for butterflies and for us, is unavoidable. Sometimes change happens to us without warning and all we can do is respond to it. Other times, we are the ones who begin it, or the ones who carry it forward. No matter the role we play, nature reminds us what matters. When we embrace change with patience, grace, and trust - accepting it as part of our own life cycle - we give ourselves the chance to grow and evolve.

Embrace.

Love,
Esme

May 11

"Knowledge"

Dear Reader,

My parents have always told me that knowledge is power. As I've grown, I've come to understand why. There is no limit to how much you can learn. Once knowledge becomes part of you, no one can take it away. It is essential and moves and shapes everything it touches. Knowledge reminds me of water.

Water covers most of our planet and is a necessity for all life. Through the water cycle, it moves constantly; shifting between gas, liquid, and solid. Water evaporates from oceans and lakes, rises into the air, condenses into clouds, and returns to the Earth as rain, snow, or ice. It flows across the land, seeps into the soil, nourishes plants, and then rises again. It is above us, around us, and beneath our feet.

Knowledge, like water, exists all around us. When we share what we know, it doesn't disappear - it changes form; growing richer as it moves from source to source.

Water links air, oceans, lands, and all living things in one cycle. Knowledge connects individuals, communities, and generations. And wherever knowledge flows, it nourishes and grows in the minds of many.

Circulate.

Love,
Esme

May 15

"Barriers"

Dear Reader,

When I watch beavers at work, I'm reminded of how progress is limitless. A beaver never assumes its lodge is finished. If the space becomes too small, it doesn't accept that as a permanent condition. It studies the structure, removes a wall, and builds outward using the same materials it already has. Beavers don't see their own creations as barriers, they see them as starting points.

Over time, we build beliefs about who we are and what we can do. Some of those beliefs protect us, but others quietly box us in. Life gives us knowledge and experience, and with them comes the ability to reassess what we've built. When we pause and look honestly at ourselves, we may realize that some limits we're facing are walls we constructed long ago.

Like the beaver, we have the tools to remove what no longer serves us and make room for growth. The moment we recognize that we are both the architect and the builder of our lives, we discover that expansion and growth are always possible.

Remove.

Love,
Esme

May 27

"Obstacles"

Dear Reader,

There are moments in life when you come face to face with an obstacle and realize you can't move past it on your own.  In those moments, it's important to remember that needing help isn't a weakness.  Sometimes, the bravest thing you can do is allow others to assist you.

Unlike many other ants, army ants don't build permanent homes.  Their colony is always on the move in search of food.  When they encounter an obstacle, they don't turn back.  They face the challenge together.

Army ants have been seen forming living bridges using their own bodies.  One ant reaches out, then another, and another; each one adding itself to the structure.  They reinforce weak spots, adjust as needed, and stay in place until the path is complete.  Once the rest of the colony has crossed, the bridge gently comes apart, and the ants continue on their journey.

We are not meant to overcome every challenge alone.  Sometimes progress requires the support of others - those willing to stand with us, steady us, and help us across.  It is okay to ask for and accept support.  Your actions will inspire others to do the same.

Overcome.

Love,
Esme

June 9

"Truth"

Dear Reader,

The cicadas have arrived. I remember reading an article about a massive emergence expected across dozens of states. At the time, I didn't know much about cicadas, so I did what I always do - I let my curiosity lead the way.

Cicadas belong to the insect family *Cicadidae*. One group in particular, the periodical cicadas, lives most of its life hidden from view. As larvae or nymphs, they remain underground for 13 to 17 years, quietly feeding and waiting.

When the time comes, they rise to the surface. The nymphs climb a nearby tree, shrub, or other vertical surface and molt, shedding their old skin. After this, winged adults emerge. Their time above ground is brief - only three or four weeks - just long enough to mate and lay eggs so that the cycle can repeat.

Cicadas can cause damage both before and after they emerge. When underground, the nymphs feed heavily on the roots of plants, which can weaken growth. After mating, females lay eggs on plants and trees, which creates scarring on crops like grapevines, citrus trees, cotton, and palms.

Watching the cicadas return reminds me that what is hidden doesn't stay hidden forever. The truth always has a way of surfacing. When something is buried too long - like the nymphs underground - it can quietly damage us at the root, weakening us as a whole. Speaking the truth may scar us on the surface, but the damage is temporary.

Honesty, even when uncomfortable, allows for growth. When the truth is brought into the light, it gives us the space to heal and the chance to start again.

Heal.

Love,
Esme

June 11

"Beyond"

Dear Reader,

Giraffes are symbols of grace, strength, and quiet determination. Their long necks are one of their most distinguishing features and allow giraffes to reach leaves, fruits, and flowers that remain untouched by others. While some animals can only feed on what grows low to the ground, giraffes can look up, stretch, and reach higher.

To reach our fullest potential, we have to be willing to extend ourselves beyond what feels familiar or comfortable. Growth doesn't happen when we only aim for what is already within reach. Sometimes, it requires us to lift our gaze and stretch toward something more.

I've learned not to be afraid of setting goals that feel slightly out of my reach. When we stretch beyond our perceived limits, we can accomplish what we set out to achieve and all of the small goals in between.

Stretch.

Love,
Esme

June 20

"Effort"

Dear Reader,

Summer has arrived, and with it comes time to slow down and spend the days with my friends. What I love most about this season is being outside - breathing in warm, fresh air and feeling the world open up around me.

The days have become long, trees are full of leaves, and flowers seem to cover every inch of open space. Fruits are ripening and are heavy on their branches. It feels as though spring has passed the baton, and summer has taken off at full speed, finishing what was carefully begun.

All of nature's planning, patience, and steady care have led to this moment. The quiet work done over time has blossomed into something vibrant and alive.

Watching this reminds me that effort matters. Whatever you choose to work toward, may you move forward with consistency and care and may the results of your dedication be as full and abundant as summer itself.

Apply.

Love,
Esme

July 5

"Direction"

Dear Reader,

Life is a journey of discovery. Along the way, we come across many paths. Some connect and carry us forward, others take us in unexpected directions, and a few end sooner than we thought they would. At times, the journey can feel confusing and overwhelming. When I feel lost, I look to the stars.

The night sky is filled with countless stars, each one different in size and brightness. At first, it can feel like too much to take in. But when you focus on just a few stars at a time and begin to connect them, patterns start to appear. Slowly, the sky reveals images; constellations that have guided people for centuries.

Sailors once used these constellations to map the sky, find their location, and determine which direction to travel. The stars became trusted reference points, helping them navigate vast and uncertain waters.

I like to think of life events the same way. Each experience on its own is a moment of learning. But when you step back and connect them, they form something meaningful; a constellation unique to you. The lessons you gather become points of reference, helping you understand where you've been, where you are, and which path you might take next.

Stars were used for navigation because they remained constant. They didn't disappear, even as everything else shifted.

While our circumstances in life may change, the lessons we learn stay with us. If we use them wisely, these lessons can help orient us and guide us forward, even when the path ahead isn't clear.

Find.

Love,
Esme

July 13

"Whole"

Dear Reader,

There are moments when a lizard loses its tail. Along its tail is a natural weak point called a fracture plane. When the tail is struck, stressed, or pulled, the muscles separate at that point and the tail breaks away. It's a startling thing to witness, but what follows is truly remarkable. In time, the lizard grows a new one.

In life we are often pulled in many directions and circumstances can leave us feeling torn or diminished. We don't have the physical ability to regenerate the way a lizard does, but I believe we have something just as powerful - a spiritual ability to restore ourselves.

That restoration begins when we understand our own wholeness. To me, wholeness means being fully present and invested in ourselves - emotionally, mentally, spiritually, and physically. When those parts of us are aligned, we stand grounded in who we are.

When we enter life's challenges with that awareness, we can choose not to let circumstances break us apart. We get to decide whether what happens to us minimizes or strengthens us. Nature reminds me that while we can't always choose our circumstances, we can choose to remain whole.

Remain.

Love,
Esme

July 18

"Vehicle"

Dear Reader,

Perhaps you will find the title of this entry ironic. For the rate at which a vehicle moves is in stark contrast to the rate at which the mammal I am about to mention moves. However, I think you will come to find the title most fitting.

Sloths have a bad reputation. They move slowly, sleep up to 20 hours a day, and spend most of their waking moments hanging quietly in the tops of trees. Because of this, they're often used as symbols of laziness and to show lack of productivity.

But a vehicle isn't only something that just moves quickly. It is anything that carries something from one place to another or helps bring something into being.

Because of their grooved hair, their stillness, and their slow movements, sloths are a home to many forms of life. Green algae, beetles, cockroaches, worms, and moths all live in their fur. Some of these organisms exist nowhere else, and others rely entirely on the sloth to complete their life cycle. In this way, a sloth is a living, breathing ecosystem; a vehicle for life itself.

This makes me think about how we can also be vehicles. Just as sloths carry life, we can carry kindness, change, love, and progress into the world. It doesn't matter how fast we move. What matters is our willingness to carry them forward.

Carry.

Love,
Esme

July 28

"Setbacks"

Dear Reader,

I've always felt a deep connection to the ocean. To me, it holds so many qualities at once: strength and gentleness, flexibility and consistency, and calm and constant movement. It reminds me that opposites can exist together in beautiful balance.

The tides are shaped by forces we don't always see. Guided by the pull of the sun and the moon, the ocean rises and falls in a steady rhythm.

We can experience our own highs and lows - moments of fullness and moments when we feel like we have been pulled backward and need to start again. Like the ocean, we are adaptable and resilient, capable of drawing on our own inner strength to lift and move ourselves forward.

When we feel down, the ocean reminds us that we can and will rise again.

Adapt.

Love,
Esme

July 31

"Presence"

Dear Reader,

When I think of a peacock, I imagine it standing still, tail feathers fanned out, colors shimmering in full view. It is completely present in the moment, unapologetic in its display.

A male peacock displays his feathers to attract a mate, and in doing so seems to declare, "This is who I am". He does not second-guess himself. His confidence is instinctual. For us, presence and confidence often require intention. We often hesitate out of fear - fear of rejection, of failure, of not being enough. And this holding back shows up not only in relationships, but in our ideas, our ambitions, and the risks we are called to take.

Fear is natural, but it was never meant to keep us small. When we choose not to show up fully, we deny ourselves the chance to discover our own depth and potential. Nature reminds me that courage is not loud or forceful; it is simply the willingness to stand as you are.

Like with the peacock, there is power in presence and beauty in authenticity. Be seen. Trust that when you offer yourself with honesty and intention, the beauty that you project will be returned to you in abundance.

Stand.

Love,
Esme

August 10

"Lens"

Dear Reader,

Back in April I read an article about the discovery of a new species of peacock spiders. The lesson that I had originally missed has now revealed itself. I now see.

Peacock spiders are tiny, brightly colored jumping spiders native to Australia. Despite their small size, they're known for their elaborate mating dances; movements full of intention and display. What shocked me most was how this new species was discovered. A photographer wasn't even looking for it. A flower was the intended subject. The spider appeared in the frame almost by accident. That made me wonder what else exists just outside of my focus.

Our eyes work like the lens of a camera. They decide what stays sharp and what fades into the background. Even though we're always looking, we don't always see. We tend to focus on what serves our interests, keeping our chosen subject clear while everything else becomes a blur.

Nature reminds me that the world is filled with extraordinary things; quiet, beautiful moments waiting to be noticed. There are lessons everywhere, if we're willing to widen our view and allow ourselves to see what we often overlook.

See.

Love,
Esme

August 18

"Voice"

Dear Reader,

The voice is a powerful thing. I try to never forget the power of my own.

The white bellbird lives in the forests of Brazil, the Guianas, Venezuela, and Trinidad and Tobago. The females blend into their surroundings with olive-colored feathers, while the males are strikingly white, marked only by a black bill and wattle. What truly sets the male white bellbird apart, though, is its call. It has the loudest bird call ever recorded.

The male white bellbird actually has two calls. The most distinct is its clear, bell-like sound, which can reach up to 125 decibels. It uses this voice with purpose: to attract a mate and ensure the continuation of its species. Nothing about its call is accidental.

Our voices are purposeful too. Each of us has a voice that is uniquely our own. We can use it to communicate, to comfort, to express ideas, to warn, to stand up for ourselves, and to speak up on behalf of others. Sometimes a louder voice is necessary, but the true power of one's voice comes from within.

It is not always how loud we speak, but what we say that allows our voice to travel far and our message to be heard.

Speak.

Love,
Esme

August 30

"Persevere"

Dear Reader,

Tardigrades are microscopic, eight-legged animals found in nearly every corner of the Earth. Because of their size, they are easy to overlook, yet their resilience is extraordinary. They endure extreme heat and cold, radiation, pressure, and long periods without water. And although their lives are seemingly quiet and unseen by most, their influence has reached far beyond the limits of a microscope. So much so, that these tiny powerhouses have inspired innovations in science and technology.

Strength, like nature, reveals itself in many forms. Physical strength is the most visible and often the most celebrated, but it is not the only kind that matters. Perseverance, discipline, patience, determination, and adaptability are strengths rooted in endurance. They can carry us through hard times and keep us going when our tasks seem too great.

Like with the tardigrade, your ability to persevere will help you withstand whatever challenges come your way. May you move forward with humility and resolve.

Triumph.

Love,
Esme

September 24

"Senses"

Dear Reader,

Nature, in her infinite wisdom, layers her presence to provide the opportunity for depth and connection. In doing so, she provides an open invitation for us to immerse ourselves in awareness and understanding of her offerings.

Throughout the natural world, animals are equipped with specialized senses that allow them to experience, navigate, and survive their environments. Bats rely on echolocation, snakes detect infrared radiation, elephants navigate by scent, bees sense magnetic fields, and octopuses perceive the world through polarized vision.

We move through nature every day, surrounded by her sights, sounds, scents, flavors, and textures, yet so often we pass by without truly noticing. Perhaps because she is always there, we have grown accustomed to her presence and take her gifts for granted. What is familiar can easily become invisible.

To reconnect with her, I think we must first change how we look at her. Slow down. Engage differently. Allow our hands to see, our breath to taste, and our ears to feel. When we shift our awareness in this way, nature will reveal herself anew - layered, generous, and endlessly magnificent.

Engage.

Love,
Esme

September 26

"Prepare"

Dear Reader,

Fall is my absolute favorite season. With a shift in color and temperature, nature reveals her depth and versatility; her quiet confidence in switching gears. She is unafraid to show another side of herself, and in doing so, she invites us to change and adapt.

Like the seasons that come before and after, nature repeats her patterns with intention, understanding that we are creatures of habit. We learn through repetition. Her visible changes become gentle markers, earthly cues that help guide our movements, rhythms, and efforts.

In this season, bears are most active. Hibernation is near, so they eat and drink continuously, storing what they need to sustain themselves through the long winter ahead.

Trees, too, begin their preparation. They highlight their leaves in brilliant color, signaling for us to add our own layers for warmth and protection just before they start shedding their own colorful canopy.

Fall teaches us about balance between inner and outer strength. Beneath her vibrant exterior, nature is quietly letting go of the excess in order to protect and nourish her core. Though she prepares for outward dormancy, she is thriving inwardly, reminding us that preservation and growth often happen beneath the surface.

Renew.

Love,
Esme

October 17

"Filter"

Dear Reader,

Sponges are among the simplest of animals. They have no nervous, digestive, or circulatory systems, yet they survive and thrive. Their bodies are porous by design, allowing water to pass freely through them; drawing in nutrients as it enters and carrying waste away as it flows back out.

Life is a vast sea of experiences. Some arrive gently, others crash in unexpectedly. Each one passes through us. As we process new experiences, we learn to discern what nourishes us mentally, emotionally, and physically. The lessons and wisdom are what we keep. The rest, the heaviness and the excess, we can choose to let go.

Like the sponge, may we filter with intention; retaining what sustains us and allowing what does not nourish us to move on.

Release.

Love,
Esme

November 21

"Phases"

Dear Reader,

I find myself drawn to the night sky. There is a quiet comfort in looking upward and tracing pinpoints of light scattered across a dark and seemingly endless space. Among all of the night's lights, the moon stands brightest. It faithfully moves through its phases; changing, yet staying constant.

During each lunar month, the moon passes through her familiar rhythm: new, waxing, full, and waning, with gentle transitions in between. Each phase arrives without resistance, flowing into the next with ease and intention. No stage competes with another and each holds its own beauty and glow.

We move through phases of personal change and growth. In these moments, remember the moon. Change is not a loss of light, only a shift in form. Every phase has purpose, and each one will carry you toward fullness once again.

Glow.

Love,
Esme

December 12

"Fear"

Dear Reader,

Everyone has fears.  I feel uncomfortable speaking in front of a large group of people and being in small spaces.  In these situations, it is easy for me to become overwhelmed.  It is also in these moments of vulnerability that I think of the puffer fish.

When threatened, a puffer fish does not flee.  Instead, it draws inward, filling itself with water and expanding its body until it appears far larger than the danger before it.  A body that once seemed small becomes formidable.

When I center myself and refuse to let fear dictate who I am, I grow beyond it.  My fear does not disappear, but it loses its power.  The puffer fish teaches us that by standing fully in yourself, you can become bigger than what you fear.

Harness.

Love,
Esme

December 27

"Experience"

Dear Reader,

This year is drawing to a close. As I turn back through the pages I've written, I pause to reflect on what they hold: what I have observed, what I have learned, and how each lesson has quietly shaped me. These reflections give me the confidence to step into the new year with greater clarity, ready to move forward with intention and momentum.

Kangaroos cannot move backward. Their powerful tails, which provide balance and support, make reverse movement difficult. At first glance this may seem restrictive, but to me it is a means to ensure progress.

Our experiences shape us and provide us with awareness and understanding, and while the moments that formed these lessons live in the past, the wisdom they provide remains with us. Experiences trail behind us like a kangaroo's tail directing our movement, offering us balance, stability, and perspective. They ground us, reminding us of where we've been, so we can stand firmly in the present and continue moving forward.

Reflect.

Love,
Esme

December 31

"Create"

Dear Reader,

It is the eve of the new year, and this is my final entry. Of all the gifts we are given in life, knowledge and love are ones that can endure. They do not go away once given. Instead, they grow, remaining with us while continuing on in others.

The word photosynthesis comes from "photo", meaning light, and "synthesis", meaning to make. It is the process by which green plants use sunlight, water, and carbon dioxide to create their own nourishment. While undergoing this process, plants release oxygen; a gift that allows other life to breathe and flourish. What is taken in becomes sustenance, and what is produced becomes life-giving.

My wish is that the knowledge and love held within these pages nourish you in the same way; that what you take in strengthens and empowers you and fills you with an energy that is sustaining, generous, and bright.

Hope.

Love,
Esme

# ABOUT THE AUTHOR

 N.K. Lazarre enjoys creating stories that connect young readers to the world around them.  When she is not out in nature or writing, she is spending time with her family near Los Angeles, California.

*From Nature By Esme* is her first novelette.

www.ingramcontent.com/pod-product-compliance
Lightning Source LLC
Chambersburg PA
CBHW050907180626
46814CB00007B/2927